TRAPPED

SOPHIE McKENZIE

Illustrated by
MELANIA BADOSA

Barrington Stoke

Published by Barrington Stoke
An imprint of HarperCollins*Publishers*
Westerhill Road, Bishopbriggs, Glasgow, G64 2QT

www.barringtonstoke.co.uk

HarperCollins*Publishers*
Macken House, 39/40 Mayor Street Upper,
Dublin 1, DO1 C9W8, Ireland

First published in 2023

ISBN 978-1-80090-248-0

10 9 8 7 6 5 4 3 2

Printed and Bound in the UK using 100% Renewable Electricity
at Martins the Printers Ltd

For Jodie Hodges

CHAPTER 1

The show was over. The old people had loved it. The twenty-five teenagers who made up the Hightop Youth Singers stood in the hall of the retirement home, waiting to leave.

"The bus will be here in a few minutes!" Miss Griffin called from the front door. "Please wait quietly!"

Hailey Jones was fed up. She was with her friends, Rosie and Samira, at the back of the line. Hailey was watching everyone chatter away. Well, she was mostly watching Kit, a few people along from her. She'd had a crush on Kit for ages. It was partly the way his wavy hair flopped over his eyes. And partly that big grin of his, which lit up his whole face when he spoke.

"No way, Samira!" Rosie laughed as she held up her phone. "Look at this photo!"

Rosie and Samira had been arguing all day about whose dog was the cutest.

"Puh-lease!" Samira groaned. "Check out the ears on my Lexi."

Rosie and Samira carried on arguing. Hailey tuned them out. She inched a bit closer to Kit. Two weeks ago at singing practice, he'd spent the whole time making silly faces at her across the room to see if she'd giggle. He'd even said something about going to a party together at the weekend. She'd really thought he liked her.

But then Bex Bickerton had joined the Hightop Youth Singers, and Kit had totally lost interest in Hailey.

"You sounded awesome in the last song."

Kit was talking to Bex right now. Of course he

was. Everyone wanted to talk to Bex. She was

the new star of their show – the only one able

to hit the high notes that made audiences gasp

and cheer. Plus, she was pretty with sleek dark hair, great big eyes and huge curly eyelashes.

Hailey knew she was being mean, but she didn't like Bex. Or the way everyone else thought she was so great.

"Do you really think I sounded all right, Kit?" Bex blushed as she asked.

It looked as if Bex had a big crush on Kit. Just like Hailey did.

Hailey looked down at her shoes. She felt dull and boring and totally down in the dumps. If Bex liked Kit, Hailey didn't stand a chance with him.

"The bus is here now! Let's go!" Miss Griffin clapped her hands to make everyone listen. "Come along, we're already late."

Hailey plodded along with everyone else, her hands deep in her pockets.

The Hightop Youth Singers was a local group that performed songs from musicals. Bex had only joined them two weeks ago, but everyone said it was like she'd been with the group for ever. They all went on about what a great singer she was and how she was so sweet and friendly.

Well, it wasn't very sweet and friendly to take Kit away from Hailey.

"Everyone onto the bus! Quick as you can!" Miss Griffin called. She opened the front door of the retirement home and a gust of cold air blew inside. Hailey tugged her jacket around her. It was the middle of November – cold and dark – and the end-of-term holidays were still a long way off.

As Hailey followed the others to the door, Mrs Pozinski, the manager of the retirement home, came panting up. She pushed past Hailey and went up to Bex and Kit.

"I *had* to tell you." She beamed at Bex. "Your singing is *very special*." Mrs Pozinski put her hand over her heart as if she was swelling with pride. "I, myself, used to perform in musicals when I was young, and I can tell you have an outstanding talent."

Hailey gritted her teeth. Nobody had ever said that about *her*.

"Yeah, Bex is amazing," Kit said, with his big grin.

"Oh, er, right, thanks," Bex said. She sounded awkward and bored. Like she was fed up with compliments from stupid strangers and just wanted to get back to chatting with handsome Kit.

Hailey walked past them and went outside. The air was cold and a light drizzle was falling.

Feeling the misty damp on her face, Hailey pulled up the hood of her jacket and headed across the tarmac towards the bus. It was only 5.30 p.m. but already dark and gloomy.

The inside lights of the bus were on and the engine rumbling. Miss Griffin was up by the door, waving her arms as she ushered people on board.

"Hurry up, everyone!" she cried. "We want to get on our way before the storm sets in." She looked up and down the road in an anxious way.

The retirement home was set at the top of a cliff overlooking the sea. A steep zig-zag

road led down to the town where most of the members of the singing group lived.

Hailey joined the end of the line getting on the bus. The rain fell harder and the wind blew stronger, cold against Hailey's cheeks. Up ahead of her, Rosie and Samira were arguing about whether Labrador or spaniel puppies were cuter. There was a time when Hailey would have joined in, but right now, thanks to Bex, she felt too depressed.

"Come *on*, please!" Miss Griffin called. "Kit! Bex! Hurry, we need to get going *now*!"

CHAPTER 2

Hailey kept walking to the end of the bus. She pushed past Seb and Stan, who were standing by the emergency exit halfway down the bus. They were giggling over something on Stan's phone.

Seb and Stan were always messing about. A few weeks ago, they'd got hold of some tomato-ketchup sachets, squeezed them all over the back seat and said it was blood. Ever since then, Miss Griffin had made everyone sit in the front half of the bus. But today she was too busy getting everyone on board to notice where anyone put themselves.

Hailey swung herself into the seat that ran along the back of the bus. She looked up. Kit was walking towards her, a huge grin on his face. For a second, Hailey thought he was beaming at her and sat up to smile back, her stomach flipping over with excitement.

But then Kit turned round to say something to the person behind him. It was Bex. Of course. She looked across at Hailey and, for a second, the girls' eyes met.

Bex frowned.

Hailey looked away.

"Let's sit here," Kit said, pointing to the row
in front of Hailey.

Hailey bit her lip. Had Kit even seen she was there? Bex looked a bit awkward and tugged off her coat.

"Is it OK if we sit here?" she asked Hailey.

Hailey scowled at her. Kit laughed. "You're so sweet, Bex. Hailey doesn't mind where we sit, do you, Hailey?" He winked at her, like he'd said something hilarious.

Hailey's face burned as she looked down at her lap. At the front of the bus, Miss Griffin had finished counting everyone on board. "Sit down!" she cried. "Everyone *sit down!*"

Bex and Kit slid into their seats.

"Do you take singing lessons?" Kit was asking. "Your voice is *so* amazing."

Hailey jammed her headphones over her ears, the music turned up loud. She didn't want to have to listen to Kit and Bex chatting.

The bus set off, turning slowly onto the steep road down the cliffside. The rain lashed against the windows. Hailey couldn't see much outside.

On one side of the narrow, twisty road were big trees. Their branches swayed to and fro in the wind. On the other side was a scary drop down the cliffside to the dark rocks and sea below. Hailey closed her eyes and turned up her music even louder. She couldn't wait to get home.

With a jolt, the bus bucked. Hailey's eyes shot open. The sound of glass smashing and metal crunching rose above her music. What on earth was that?

Oh no!

A couple of rows ahead of her, just in front of where Bex and Kit were sitting, something huge and hard was slamming down through the roof. As Hailey ripped off her headphones, she heard screams all around her. Hailey realised she was screaming too.

The brakes screeched as the bus spun. Hailey couldn't scream any more – her throat hurt. She was terrified. The bus slid and slipped along the wet road, then stopped dead. The engine cut out.

Hailey gripped the edge of the seat in front of her. She couldn't believe what she was looking at.

Just a couple of rows ahead, the enormous branch of a tree had crashed through the roof of the coach and crushed the seats, filling the bus from one side to the other.

CHAPTER 3

Hailey stared at the huge branch. At the
leaves and smaller branches poking out of it
and the twisted metal of the seats where it
had landed.

Thank goodness no one had been sitting
there when the branch crashed through the
roof.

The emergency lights had come on and they gave off a soft glow, like a night-light. Bex and Kit crawled out of their seats and stood up. Hailey looked down the bus.

They were the only three people on this side of the tree. Everyone else was up at the front of the bus. Screams and shouts filled the air. Hailey's heart pounded. She stood up very slowly, shaking all over.

Like her, Bex and Kit were staring at the thick branch. It filled the bus ahead of them, blocking their way to the front.

"Are you all right?" Hailey asked.

The other two nodded. Rain pattered on the leaves and twigs. They could still hear everyone at the front of the bus screaming and yelling.

Kit kept looking at the huge branch. "It must have got torn off in the storm," he said, his face pale and his voice full of shock. "I've never seen anything like it."

"What about *you*, Hailey?" Bex asked. "Are you OK?"

"I'm fine," Hailey answered. Then she went on, "I mean, I'm not hurt. Do you think the others know we're back here?"

"We need to make sure they do!" Bex said, then shouted, "Help!"

"Help!" Hailey and Kit joined in.

But no one could hear them because of all the yells from the front of the bus.

"Everyone off the bus!" they heard Miss Griffin shout. "Seb, help me with the driver."

"Come on," Hailey said, "we need to get off too." She glanced at the tree. In the dim light it was hard to make out if there was any way past it. "Maybe we can squeeze over the branches."

"I don't—" Bex started. Before she could finish, the bus gave a sickening groan and slid backwards. The three of them lost their balance. The bus was now on a slant. Hailey had to grip the back of the seat in

front of her to stay upright. What on earth
was happening?

"Everyone off *now!*" Miss Griffin shouted
up ahead. Hailey could hear her panic. "Jump
down to the ground before the bus tilts any
further!"

"We have to make them hear us!" Kit yelled.

"Help!" Bex shouted. *"HELP!"*

Hailey slowly turned her head to look through the back window of the bus. All she could see was the darkness of the cliff below. At the very bottom, everything was black, apart from the odd flash of white, which she knew came from the tips of waves crashing against the rocks.

"Oh no!" Her voice was a whisper. "We're right on the edge!"

Another slip of the wheels backwards and the bus would slide over the cliff. They would fall all the way down to their deaths.

CHAPTER 4

The end of the bus hung over the edge of the cliff. Hailey pointed through the back window. "Look!" she shouted.

"Oh!" gasped Kit.

Bex peered down to the dark rocks below. "Everyone getting off up front must have shifted the bus's weight," she said. "They've tipped us backwards."

"Never mind how it happened," Hailey said. "We need to find a way off this bus before it falls all the way down the cliff."

The three of them stared at each other in the dim light. The emergency strip lighting on the floor made gloomy shadows across the seats. Rain was still falling onto the tree branch through the hole it had made in the roof.

Hailey blew out shakily, trying to calm the panic that filled her chest. She could still hear the yells and shouts of their friends – but the sounds were further away. They must all be outside the bus.

"Help!" Kit was shouting again, but she could tell that he didn't expect anyone to answer.

"I'm sure they'll work out we're missing in a second," Hailey said.

"We're the only ones left on the bus." Bex stared out of the back window again. "I'm scared to move in case that tips the bus even more and … and …"

"… and it slides all the way over the edge," Hailey finished. "I know."

"Well, we *have* to move," Kit insisted. He turned towards the front part of the bus and pointed at the huge branch that blocked their way. "We have to find a way past that so we can get out the door."

"Maybe it will be OK so long as we move slowly and carefully," Hailey said.

"Right," Bex agreed. "No sudden jerks or leaps."

Hailey took out her phone and, with trembling fingers, switched on the torch app.

The branch that had crashed through the ceiling ran the whole way across the bus, filling it from one side to the other. The main branch was massive, while the smaller branches and the thick clumps of leaves that stuck out from them reached from high above the bus roof right down to the floor. Hailey stared at a bit of one of the seats, crushed and twisted.

She shuddered.

"I can't see a way past," Bex muttered.

"But there *has* to be," Kit said. He inched closer to the tree. Bex followed, right behind him. The light from their phones shone off the bark and leaves as they looked more carefully to see if they could get through.

Hailey bit her lip. Bex was right. The branch was too big. The way to the front part of the bus was completely blocked off.

"We're trapped," Kit said.

"Can you hear that?" Bex whispered.

Hailey frowned, concentrating on listening.

"Hailey! Kit! Bex!" It was Miss Griffin, shouting over the noise of the storm. "Are you there?"

"Hey!"

"Hello!"

"We're here!"

The three of them yelled together.

"We're OK!" Hailey went on. "But we're
stuck."

"Just sit tight!" Miss Griffin called. "The emergency services are on their way. They'll get you out."

"OK!" Hailey and Kit called back.

"That's a relief," Kit said, pushing his hair off his face.

But at that moment the bus lurched backwards again.

Hailey shrieked in shock and terror. "What the—?"

"We're sliding over the edge!" Bex yelled.

Hailey stared at her. Once the back wheels were over the edge, there'd be nothing stopping the entire bus from hurtling down the sheer drop below.

"What do we do?" Kit shouted. "There's no way out!"

CHAPTER 5

The bus teetered. Hailey's stomach lurched.
Any minute they would plummet down the
cliff and crash onto the rocks below.

She stared at the sign by the back window. It said: "Emergency Exit". There was a box next to it with a hammer to break the glass. It didn't matter. There was no way to escape out the back. Below them was that sheer drop to the dark waters under the cliff.

Kit was looking at the sign too. Suddenly, he grabbed Hailey's arm.

"Isn't there another emergency exit halfway up the bus?" he asked.

"Yes!" Hailey pointed along the rows of seats to where she'd seen Seb and Stan when they first got on the bus. "If we could just get past the tree, then—"

"But we *can't* get past the tree," Bex wailed.

"What are we going to do?" Kit cried.

Hailey shone her torch around the bus. The light glinted off the windows and lit up the rain still driving down outside.

"Let's break *that*," Hailey said, grabbing the emergency hammer and pointing to a side window with solid ground beyond it. "We can jump out there."

The three of them tiptoed over to the window. Hailey drove the hammer against the glass.

Wham!

Again.

The window cracked but didn't break. They each took a turn, but though the crack got deeper, the glass didn't give way.

Hailey looked up. Just above the window was a rack to store bags and cases.

"Grab hold of the rack," she said, scrambling onto the seat and reaching up above her head. "Swing from it. Swing back and then forward and kick the glass out."

"OK." Bex climbed up beside Hailey. She looked grim but set on what Hailey had said to do.

"Come on!" said Kit, jumping up on Hailey's other side.

As he moved, the shift in weight made the bus groan.

"Hurry!" Bex urged.

"On my count!" Hailey said. "One." She gripped the top of the rack. Bex and Kit followed suit. "Two." The three of them swung back at exactly the same time, ready to swing forward against the glass. "*Kick!*"

Hailey kicked the window as hard as she could. The crack in the glass lengthened.

"Again!" Kit called.

The three of them swung back as the bus tilted and lurched. It was about to fall. Hailey gripped the rack and kicked hard.

Wham!

The glass shattered, letting in a gust of cold night air.

"Jump!" Hailey yelled.

The bus started to slide.

The dark sky rushed past as she hurled herself out into the night.

CHAPTER 6

Hailey dived through the bus window and out into the night. The hard ground slammed up to meet her. She lay in the dark, her cheek pressed into the cold earth, unable to move, unable to breathe.

Kit was sprawled on the ground nearby. He was panting for breath, his eyes open wide with shock.

Rain poured down. A huge thud echoed up
from the bottom of the cliffs as the bus crashed
onto the rocks below.

A second later it exploded.

Boom!

Hailey gasped as a fireball flared, lighting up the trees and bushes. For a split second, Hailey saw Bex slumped over on a ledge of rock a few metres below them. Then the fireball shrank back, and they were in darkness once more.

High above her, Hailey could hear yells – though the wind was too strong for her to hear the exact words. She lifted her head. She had no idea how far they were from the place where the bus had first skidded, but it felt like a long way. Rain trickled down her face and she wiped it out of her eyes. She was already soaked through.

"Are you all right?" Kit asked, sitting up.

"I'm fine." Hailey patted down her arms and legs to make sure she really was. She was sore where she had landed on her side, but she was OK.

"Hey!" she called up the cliff. Then, more loudly, "*Help!*"

She waited, but no one answered.

"They can't hear us." Kit sighed. He began to shout too. "Help! We're down here! *Help!*"

They yelled together, but it was no use.

Hailey took her phone and shone a light down to Bex. The other girl was still lying, slumped, on the ledge of rock.

"I think Bex is hurt," she said.

Kit pushed his wet hair off his forehead to look. "I'm going to go for help. You stay here with Bex. We can't leave her on her own."

Hailey didn't much like the idea of staying on the wet, cold cliffside, but she knew Kit was right. "Of course," she said.

Kit set off, crawling over the earth like a spider. He was quickly out of sight up the hill.

Hailey sat in the dark, the rain still drumming down. Her hands were sticky from the muddy earth, her whole body cold and damp. Now her eyes were used to the darkness, she could see that the cliffside above her was very steep. She hoped Kit would be OK making the climb to the top.

Suddenly, she heard the sound of someone crying. Hailey shone her light down to Bex. She was sitting up now, crouched on the ledge of rock, sobbing.

"Hey!" Hailey called. "Bex? Are you all right?"

Bex looked up, holding her hand across her face to cut out the glare of Hailey's torch. "I've hurt my ankle!" she cried out.

"Just stay where you are," Hailey yelled. "Kit's gone for help!"

Bex didn't answer. She nodded, then shrank back, still crying. Her ankle must be hurting a lot.

Hailey didn't know what to do next. Up until a few minutes ago, she wouldn't have cared much about Bex's feelings. But now, after nearly dying on the bus, it seemed silly to have been so angry about Kit liking Bex. After all, how could Bex have known how she, Hailey, felt about him?

Hailey thought she'd shuffle down to where Bex was crouched. The earth felt cold and wet and slippery under her body.

"Hi," she said awkwardly as she got near Bex.

Bex looked up, tears glinting in her eyes. "Hello," she sniffed.

"Is your ankle really sore?" Hailey asked.

Bex shook her head. "Only when I put weight on it." She wasn't wearing a coat, and she was shivering really badly.

Hailey peeled off her jacket and slipped it around Bex. It was soaking wet but would still be better than nothing, she thought.

"Thanks," Bex said.

The wind drove rain into Hailey's face. She sat back, leaning against the side of the cliff to get a little shelter from the storm.

"Why didn't you climb up with Kit?" Bex asked, wiping her face. "You could be up there now with everyone else, instead of down here with me."

Hailey said. "I ... we ... didn't want to leave you all alone."

Bex met her gaze. "Really?" she said. Her voice wobbled and more tears leaked from her eyes. "Thank you."

"It'll be OK," Hailey said. She wasn't really sure it would be, but she needed to comfort Bex. "Kit will let everyone know we're here, and I'm sure someone will come and rescue us – and look after your ankle."

"I'm not crying because of my ankle ... or the crash," Bex said. "Or not just those things anyway." She brushed away the tears and rain from her face, and Hailey saw the muddy streaks on her cheeks.

"So ..." Hailey frowned. "So ... what else is upsetting you?"

"It's just ..." Bex shrugged. "You're being so nice and ... and I thought you didn't like me."

"Oh." Hailey felt awkward. "That's ... but ..." Why on earth was Bex bothered about Hailey liking her? Everyone, including Kit, adored her. "*Everyone* likes you," she said firmly.

Bex frowned. "Do you think? Everyone's been really nice since I arrived, but ... but it's hard to know." She sighed. "This is the fifth time we've moved house in two years, and I keep starting in new singing groups and trying to fit in, and it's always so, *so* hard."

Hailey stared at her. She hadn't even thought for a second that it might be hard for Bex to be new. "Are you serious?" she said. "Of *course* you fit in. For one thing, you have an amazing voice."

"But that's not *me*," Bex pointed out. "I mean, it's lovely when people say nice things about my singing, but it's also embarrassing, and it makes me think that's the only reason people like me and ..." She looked away, a mix of tears and rain glinting on her cheek in the moonlight. "Sometimes people don't like the way I sing well. You know, when I come into a new group, some people feel like I've taken over a bit and don't like me because of it."

Hailey was glad it was dark so Bex couldn't see her blushing.

"Well, Kit *definitely* likes you," Hailey said, to change the subject. "And for far more than your singing. He's *obviously* got a massive crush on you."

Bex turned to face her, frowning again. "But Kit isn't into girls like that," she said. "He's more ... into boys."

CHAPTER 7

Hailey wasn't sure she'd heard Bex right. "*What?* Kit's into *boys*? But ... but ... I thought Kit was into you."

A grin spread over Bex's face. "Into *me*? Like that? No way. Me and Kit ... we're just mates, like you and him. Kit gets on with everyone."

Hailey sat back on the cold grass. The rain was lighter now, a damp mist on her face.

"Oh," she said. She felt all muddled and a bit shocked. Then she realised – Kit had only ever just been being friendly; he hadn't ever shown or said that he fancied her. "I didn't know Kit was into boys," Hailey said.

"Yeah?" Bex said. "He doesn't make a big secret of it, so I thought everyone knew." She waited a moment before she went on. "Do you ... did *you* like him?"

"No," Hailey lied. "Course not."

"Really?"

Hailey gave a shrug. "Well, maybe I liked him a bit."

Bex smiled. "I get it," she said softly.

Hailey looked away, feeling embarrassed. Suppose Bex told Kit how she felt? The rain had stopped now, but her clothes were still damp and cold, clinging to her skin.

Bex shivered, then moved along the ledge of rock, feeling her ankle. "My foot doesn't hurt so much now. Maybe we could try climbing up the cliff?"

"OK," Hailey said. She watched Bex shift her weight and get up onto her knees. "Be careful," she began, "that ledge looks really slippery—"

"Aaagh!" Bex yelled. She lost her footing and slid over the ledge, her arms flailing. Hailey hurled herself forward, flat onto her

stomach. She grabbed Bex's wrist. Bex's bare skin was cold and damp in Hailey's fingers. It was hard to hold on to her tightly.

Bex yelled out again. She was scrabbling for somewhere to put her feet. The mud sprayed out around her as she kicked helplessly against the side of the cliff.

Hailey's arm ached with the effort of holding the other girl. She spotted a small bush down near Bex's right foot.

"Put your feet on that bush!" she shouted.

Wind whipped against their faces as Bex kicked her feet into the stiff, scrubby bit of bush.

"Don't let go of me!" she yelled, looking up at Hailey.

"I won't!" Hailey shouted back. "I promise."

Hailey shuffled back to where the ground was flatter, then tried to tug Bex towards her. She felt Bex anchor herself into the side of the cliff, using the bush as a foothold.

"Use the bush to push yourself up, back onto the ledge!" Hailey yelled.

With a shriek, Bex pushed and Hailey pulled. One final heave and Bex was over the rocky ledge.

As the girls lay panting for breath, two
emergency workers on ropes arrived next to
them. They helped the mud-soaked girls up
to the top of the cliff and wrapped them in
blankets. They were safe at last.

As a paramedic checked Bex's ankle, Hailey
noticed Kit waving at them from behind a

cordon. He was standing next to Miss Griffin, who was watching the rescue team at work.

The paramedic stepped away to fetch a bandage.

"Listen," Bex said. "I'm not going to say anything to Kit about you liking him. Maybe ..." She looked at Hailey hopefully. "Maybe the three of us could hang out together sometime?"

Hailey glanced over at Kit again. He was turning to say something to Rosie and Samira. Getting on with everyone, like Bex had said. Already, it felt easy to imagine herself joking and laughing with him too.

She looked at Bex, who was still waiting for Hailey to answer.

"Sure," Hailey said, a grin spreading across her face. And in that moment, she knew she had made a new friend.

Our books are tested
for children and young people by
children and young people.

Thanks to everyone who consulted on
a manuscript for their time and effort in
helping us to make our books better
for our readers.